Be Wee With Bea ^{Part 2}

Learn Ways to Trust

Liz O'Neill

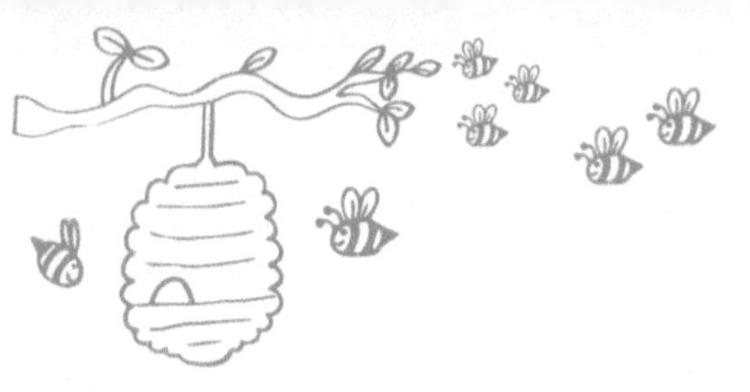

Contents

Acknowledgement

A writing friend and former classmate, Beck Fenton, suggested I check out a writing website called FanStory. I have been a member of this group of excellent writers and supportive reviewers since 2018. I have met some wonderfully helpful people in this group and am aware of how much I have improved and what a better writer I am. This is where I've been inspired and kindly coached on the books I've written. I will be forever grateful to Beck and my new writing friends, sadly too numerous to mention.

About The Author

Liz K. O'Neill, a third-generation Vermonter, spent 28 years in a religious community and has a Master's degree in Education with a Minor in Language Arts. She taught writing and literature in grades 6–10 for 20 years. She wrote curricula for her undergraduate and graduate courses at her local college, where she taught for seven years.

At that same time, she volunteered and was later employed for approximately 30 years in a women's advocacy shelter, where she developed an extensive educational website called 'Imbalance in Relationships.' She recently retired from serving as a mental health worker in a psychiatric or substance abuse treatment program. She is very interested in archaeology and reads novels based on digs and discoveries.

She has currently completed several books, including "Be Wee With Bea: Learn Ways to Cope," and is currently working on the third installment of the book series. She has also completed two other books: One is called "Traffic," which features the rescue of 10 Native American teens from a trafficking operation. Another, titled "Tor," features power spots in England and deviates to a time travel vortex in a 16th-century monastery.

The last one which she began more than twenty years ago and is called "A Particular Friendship," is about her time before entering the convent, her time there, and her life since leaving the convent.

Dedication

Maureen Kai Buskirk provided me with the courage and inspiration to write the second installment of this series. These episodes are about all of our 'puppies,' as we call the dogs. In this suspenseful, touching, and humorous book, she plays Doolie the wise bear. Maureen has since passed and joined all of our puppies at the Rainbow Bridge.

Note To The Reader

If you liked Be Wee With Bea Part 1*****This is the book for you

If you enjoy solving mysteries*****This is the book for you

If you have trust issues*****This is the book for you

If you like taking risks*****This is the book for you

If you like lots of dogs*****This is the book for you

If you want to know how to make friends*****This book is for you

If you have experienced losses*****This book is for you

If you want to enjoy reading a really good book*****This book is for you

If you are a student who needs a chapter book*****This book is for you

Introduction

If you have already been doing your strolling exercise with Bea, then you know that the main character, Bea the wee bear, is very easy to identify with. She is a sort of universal figure, experiencing the total of all readers' joys, companionships, anxieties, brokenness, fears, darkness, and great losses, to name a few.

She is still a bit of an overeater and a severe sugar addict who binges on exercise while bingeing on honey, her "be good to myself" treat. She behaves this way when she is stressed.

She continues to have even more interesting, entertaining adventures with her two dear friends, Scruffles and Sweet Puppy. She consults with Timothy, the clay pot-making beaver, about the furniture carving, and with Willow, the caring tree, who is always there for anyone who needs to talk.

Bea meets Doolie, the wise bear, another mom to four puppies; Benny, Zoe, Annie, and Maddie. This addition to the plot, as you might imagine, brings even more unusual missions requiring Bea to do her brain exercise.

Great investigation exercises will surely ensue. Each of these new characters has their own story, which we will slowly learn.

In case you were concerned, Bea will not have to share her "be good to myself" treat with Doolie, who long ago performed her brain and investigation exercises to solve the food problem. With that many in her brood, she had to be Doolie the wise bear.

Once again, Bea, the wee bear, invites you to continue reading on in this book that is intended for both children and adults. Please join all of them in the Be Wee With Bea rigorous exercises.

Preface

Some of you have already met Bea the wee bear, Scruffles, Sweet Puppy, Timothy, Willow, and Scruffles' friend, Harriet. But this time, think of it as a new meeting, a new adventure.

We tend to think, "Oh, I know this person. I pretty well know all about them. I know how they're going to react to things." If you are getting together with a friend, waking up beside someone, or going to work, are you able to anticipate how things will go with that friend or coworker? Can you guess the adventures that you will experience because of them?

In this set of adventures, Bea still does her rigorous exercise program of stepstooling, fine motor weight lifting, toe touching, floor touching, and running in place. We will learn more about her newly discovered exercises.

As she discovered those exercises, she became aware of what "being wee" really means. These, of course, will be continued here; however, some new ones will be introduced.

You will also meet Doolie and her brood—Benny, Zoe, Annie, and Maddie—and the new adventures and lessons they afford the wee bear to discover. If you do the brain exercise that Bea suggests, you will be able to wisely choose which other exercises you would like to begin or continue to practice. Bea hopes you have already begun engaging in many of them.

Bea invites you to join her in a strolling exercise and see where it leads. Reacquaint yourself with her and her old friends, and meet many new ones, too. And above all, learn to be wee with Bea.

Chapter 1

SOMETHING SLINKLNG

Bea woke up early and quietly did her stepstooling exercises, not dropping a drip of honey and certainly not crashing clay pots, empty or full. The last thing she wanted to do was to wake Scruffles or Sweet Puppy.

Neither of them had been able to sleep well the night before due to the terrifying thunder and lightning storms. Scruffles had remained at his usual storm station, the cave opening. Bea and Sweet Puppy huddled together and assumed their well-learned defense position—cowering in the furthest corner of the room in their cave home.

Just as they had believed things were clear, a new storm bullied its way in, and there was another louder crash. Finally, just like fireworks, there was a deafening sizzle and bang. It seemed endless until they could finally trust the silence.

Maybe the brave Maine Coon Cat thought if a spear of lightning headed their way, he could reach up and knock it out of the air, the way he could a rubber ball pushed by the wind rolling toward him. He was very good at his game of knocking a bright orange maple leaf out of the air as it fell from a tree.

Bea, herself, felt quite ragged. By the time this worn-out wee bear got onto the designated path for her strolling exercise, the sun was rising and warming the land. If the temperatures are just right, there is something that predictably appears at the beginning and end of the day. They are actually clouds hanging out just above the grasses, hills, cliffs, mountains, waters, and trees. And this is where our first adventure begins.

What an eerie sight. Strange silhouettes played off the glare in the mist. Once more, her strolling exercise must halt. The wee bear knew she needed to do her notice and investigation exercises. The sun had begun to find its way over the treetops, through the leaves and fir boughs. Because it was so hazy and off in the distance, the puzzled bear could not make out what she was looking at. It seemed to be floating over the land, all in one unit.

She was only able to watch it from a poor angle. Whatever she was squinting at was distorted by the fog. The front part of this creature seemed to reach the tops of some trees. The last part of it was closer to the ground. It had one fluffy head and had a hippity-skip rhythm as it moved along across the panorama.

The rate at which this eleven-legged mass has moved could not be calculated. By using the background of the brush as a gauge, she could tell it was indeed on the move. She had no idea what it was, and it made her fear grow very fast.

That was enough strolling exercise for Bea for this part of the day. She would have to do her brain exercise without the chance to do investigation exercises.

As she strolled slowly and pensively toward home, she did her brain exercise. She'd never seen anything like that. Was it just a distortion caused by the rising sun's rays wavering through the fuzzy fog?

But it was moving. Would the mist mysteriously move like that? What kind of blurred creature was that, slinking slowly into her unbelieving sights with its eleven legs and a hippity-hip at its tail end?

She noticed that the disturbing creature didn't really have a tail. It had a tiny ball stuck to it where a tail should have been. It reminded her of the ball Scruffles had found.

However, she didn't think it was the same thing. By then, the creature had faded into the mist and was gone. She did know that she was not going to go near or mention that thing to Scruffles or Sweet Puppy until she did more brain exercises. They have had enough fearful problems and don't need any more disturbances in this part of their happier lives.

Chapter 2

EVERYTHING IN BALANCE

Bea had discovered that she actually performed best when she practiced her routine exercises. It made her feel more confident in herself. She could also make time for her stepstooling exercise and her "be good to myself" treat.

Many wonderful things had been discovered because of her strolling exercise. With the most recent discovery upsetting her, it helped to reflect on whom she'd met on those adventures. There was a great deal to learn. She found friends and happiness.

She'd met that ragged raccoon cat who filled her life with such joy. They'd gotten off to a rough start, but they acted like the rocks that tumbled in the river until they were smooth.

Their rough times were smoothed out by talking things through. Hardest of all, Bea had to do her humble exercise. That proud little bear had to admit that her "trying to make things happen her way" exercise did not work very well. In fact, it did not work at all. Not one bit.

On another fortunate stroll, Bea met a poor little bedraggled creature who'd been wandering the streets for who knows how long. She was missing the hair on her hind legs and looked terribly depressed. Bea had even sung a song to her to get her to come join her and Scruffles.

An appreciative wee one, Bea realized that, had she not met Timothy, the beaver, along one of these wonderful paths that led to Timothy's pond, she would have had no furniture or clay bowls. She used those perfectly formed bowls for her golden honey, which her mom taught her was her "be good to myself" treat.

She would not have been able to do her "Be Wee With Bea" exercises, which began with her stepstooling exercise, but one thing led to the another. First, she would have to do her weightlifting exercise in order to carry her clay pots filled with honey down her steps. This made it possible for the wee hungry bear to enjoy her "be good to myself" treat.

During this time, she would practice more of her brain and notice exercises. She realized everything leads to something else and then twirls back around. That must be how problems get solved. This reminded her of the child's toy her mom had found for her. It had a little car with it that went up a little path and then could twirl back down to the ground where it began.

She hardly ever forgot that continuing her humble exercise helped many difficulties to work out right. As long as she did her talk to the maker, everything would stay in balance. A perfect example of keeping things in balance was when she met Willow on one of her paths.

Bea discovered the wonderful exercise that Willow practiced, always being there for the sad children, waiting to give them hope. Unlike most, Willow was able to listen without any distractions. What a gift she has given everyone by listening. She helped Bea learn how to listen better to others. Bea did find concentrating on listening very difficult and wondered how Willow could do it. She thought she'd ask her someday.

She had enjoyed her Bea's Golden Path for as long as she could remember. Then it changed so much that she couldn't even recognize it. Bea never felt good about what had happened.

She knew as always, that talking to the maker of golden paths and the maker of everything helped her feel so much calmer. Many of her fears went away, and eventually everything twirled around to be okay. She kept telling herself that everyone would be safe if she talked to the maker of the creatures of the fog. She planned to do that soon.

Chapter 3

THINGS CRACKING

Many times on her strolling exercises, Bea had walked a distance from that terrible area that led to Bea's Golden Path. She had never seen the change taking place. She realized this was because she had been too busy thinking about her wonderful footprints and the golden part of the path that used to be there. She wondered what else she had missed over time because she hadn't done her important notice exercise.

Walking cautiously toward the black path, she promised herself that she would do more of her notice exercise. This was difficult, and she had to make her courage bigger than her sadness. She felt such heaviness, and her bad memories came pouring back. The sacred place in front of her used to be golden, like the color of her "be good to myself" treat.

She had discovered it. So many leaves have fallen on a beautiful path of golden dirt that held her footprints. She fondly remembered darting in and out of the path and joyously discovering that her pawprints were still there. Some even had her claw and paw marks.

Her thoughts had turned to blackness, just like the awfulness that had been poured over her footprints. She remembered the tracks left by all of the creatures who had the honor and pleasure to walk Bea's Golden Path. That whole nightmare was rushing back upon the smell of something terrible, and Scruffles ran with her to see what was going on.

She wasn't sure she could continue her investigation exercise or her notice exercise. It hurt too much. Bea's Golden Path was gone, no longer there. Why was she even visiting it? Then she heard that soft humming of bees that always comforted her, and it gave her courage to go closer.

Bea thought of the pattern of weather her mom had told her about. She remembered feeling severe cold and then oppressive heat. The coolest place was her cave home. Her mom said this caused the black to melt and crack. There were wonderful giant cracks all along what used to be the black path.

Now, it was a path of cracks. Bea was elated and began doing a drumming dance, hoping to make more cracks. Counting as her mother had taught her, many little trees were poking up. They reminded her of the ones she and Timothy, the wood carving, clay pot making, tree planting beaver, had put into clay pots. Each crack seemed to have life peeking out from the darkness into the light of the warm sun.

She was sure that Timothy had not been there to plant anything. She knew for certain that she had not stepped foot, paw, or claw on this spot, so it must be the maker of Golden Paths and the maker of trees of all kinds that had planted them. She still didn't know if it had all been done by the same maker. But just in case, she did her talk to the maker of all things anyway. Bea, the wee bear, felt somehow that would take care of the whole thank you thing. Her steppings she left indicated that it was the happiest she'd danced in a very long time.

Chapter 4

THE RAISED STONE

In spite of waking too early for her own satisfaction, Bea did her stepstooling exercise. Scruffles and Sweet Puppy watched her going up and down the stepstool to get her "be good to myself" treat. This beautiful stepstool was carved, in addition to other pieces of furniture, by Timothy, the woodcarving beaver.

After suggesting that Sweet Puppy and Scruffles do their brain exercise to reflect on how they wanted their day to go, Bea announced that she felt an urge to do her strolling exercise on Bea's Golden Path. She wanted to investigate whether any more changes had occurred.

She had such an exciting adventure last week. There were tiny trees growing through the cracks of the black stuff covering Bea's Golden Path. She never made it there that day.

As we have seen so often during her strolling exercises, when she is really doing her notice exercise, the wee bear is able to make brand new discoveries. What she stumbled upon this day, she had never seen before. It was as if it had just arrived, like someone had just put it there.

Bea knew it was old, as old as her cave home, which she was sure had been used over many long, cold sleeps with families living in it.

She loved her cave home, it was just right. It was fairly new to her. She had only lived there for a few cold, snowy long sleep times with her "be good to myself" treat. That was before she met Scruffles. And now, many icy, dark days had passed since that strange meeting of two friends who had very little in common.

Later, she met another who was maybe a little bit more like her. Scruffles, Sweet Puppy, and their mom, Bea, the caring, sometimes a little too much, wee bear had become a wonderful trio.

She became aware that her thoughts had wandered. They were nice thoughts, but they had drifted away from what she was seeing at this moment. She has plenty of trouble doing her focus exercises. This situation called for a rigorous effort.

She just knew that there was something special about what she was looking at. It was flat on the top and round on the bottom. But it wasn't just a big stone sitting on the ground; it was on top of smaller stones. The top had a very faint carving in it that looked like the biggest bird Bea had ever seen.

As she stepped back, she realized the whole rock was shaped like a bird, and as she circled this wonder, she knew she was right. It still looked like a bird wherever she stood. She wondered what it was like underneath. The amazed wee bear could not believe her eyes as she got down on her knees.

There were two particular stones underneath that took her breath away. One was a carving of a face that resembled Scruffles. Bea was quite certain that this was the face of a cat that had been around long before any raccoon cats.

The other, even stranger to her eyes, looked like the giant form of her friend Snakely. However, this also had giant carved wings sloping down its sides. She remained there for a while, as still as she could, admiring how that carved stone was the color of snow.

She remembered that same striking white color in some of the stones placed in the walls along this path. She wondered if the stone builders and carvers were the same. Maybe they had spent time doing their brain exercises and their talk to the maker of stones in some of the nearby caves.

She pictured them joyfully fishing from the Singing Stones river, where she, Scruffles, and Sweet Puppy visit daily. She has to tell them what a special place their river is. She heard the softest breeze she'd ever heard before, which reminded her to talk to the maker of everything. With a bird in the background drumming on a tree, she left this memorable spot, lightly touching the ground in a dance.

Chapter 5

SHADOWS ON THE WALL

As the sun set behind Bea, it shimmered through the leaves of the trees. She was returning from a meaningful strolling exercise. She raised her arms, relieved that she had not seen the mist creature earlier that morning. You may remember that at the beginning of our story, she once again had her exercise interrupted by a strange creature moving through the fog. Her next thought as she entered her cave home was to do her sweet stepstooling exercise, where she went up and down her step stool carrying her pots of honey, which she enjoyed as her "be good to myself" treat. This humble wee bear wanted to talk to the maker of everything, in an appreciative tone, about her happy day.

We have learned along with Bea that things don't always go the way we plan. We sometimes see something, but it doesn't really click in our brain. It's as if our eyes see it but not our brain. The movement was there in the corner of her left wee bear eye. Her brain did not want to see it. She did her pretend exercise.

Her fears were growing, and the fifty bees were swirling around inside her. It must have been peeking out from the cave opening with its head crooked. The sun shining behind it caused its shadow on the wall. She wondered if this was a baby of the larger fifteen-legged fog creature, which she had seen a couple of sunrises ago.

This creature had twelve legs. Standing close to Sweet Puppy and Scruffles, she dared not move a paw. It was her responsibility to protect them. She hoped her silent gasping had not been heard by anyone, especially the creature. It could not know she had seen it or how frightened she was. She needed to do her investigation exercise.

The stepstooling exercise would have to wait. She had to peek. She'd be quick about it. She jerked her head to try to catch a glimpse of the new, smaller creature. All she saw were Sweet Puppy and Scruffles standing in their favorite spot. There was nothing beyond them at the opening of the cave.

She hesitated to alarm them, as they already had enough problems and bad memories. Turning back to her shelves of honey pots, she spied on the wall again. She spun 'round toward the opening. Just Sweet Puppy and Scruffles. Back around. Still there. Whirling back and forth. The creature. Sweet Puppy and Scruffles. The creature.

She couldn't take it. She had to get back to her stepstooling exercise in spite of this unsettling situation. She also worried that Sweet Puppy and Scruffles would ask her why she was just standing there frozen.

Bea would do her brain exercise, quieting herself as she had some of her "be good to myself" treat. And not a word to either of them about this would come from her honey-covered lips.

Chapter 6

ANOTHER SILHOUETTE IN THE MIDST

There it was again. Bea thought maybe it would have been better if she had waited until the sun had fully risen. But this one was different than the one she had seen several sunrises ago. Bea tried as hard as she could to keep looking at the new mist creature in her midst. This one was shorter, with a very weirdly shaped head, and moved faster than the other. There was no hippitty-skip at the end like the other. It meant there was more than one kind.

She again debated whether she should tell Scruffles and Sweet Puppy about these strange sightings. She wanted so much to turn away yet could not take her eyes off this mirage-like creature moving through the thick fog. She then remembered the shadow of the creature in her very cave home.

She must tell Scruffles and Sweet Puppy, and she needs to do it soon. In her mind, she sprinted away toward home while she tiptoed quietly and cautiously, full of thought, talking to the maker for help on how to calmly tell Scruffles and Sweet Puppy the whole story.

Chapter 7

SUNRISE SUNSET CREATURES

Bea was preparing to do her stepstooling exercise. Too much time had passed since she'd had her "be good to myself" treat. That meant she could enjoy the best honey. Her mom taught her to be good to herself and not to think bad thoughts about herself. She turned just in time to see shadow creature on the cave wall.

Startled, she raised her arms over her head, and screamed silently, her wee muzzle wide open. She didn't want to let Sweet Puppy and Scruffles know how great her fears had grown. It was her responsibility to keep them safe, as she'd promised when she took them into her cave home.

This creature was even more fantastic than the last cave wall creature and quite distinct from the morning sun creature. It had two large, furry, textured antennae that moved in waving motions, a fluffy tail, and ten legs. She turned quickly and once again saw only Scruffles and Sweet Puppy at her side. Spinning back, she noticed the creature had lowered its antennae.

She abruptly turned and tiptoed as fast as she could to the back of the cave. This was the safest place in which she and Sweet Puppy would cower, clinging to each other during thunder and lightning storms. The sinking feeling returned as every terrible moment flashed through her brain.

It all rushed back over her like the river's angry stream. On that most important day, she had not stopped to do her brain exercise. Regret had been her companion ever since.

The usually sweet wee bear had roughly placed poor unsuspecting Scruffles in that dark corner during his yowling episode. And what a time she'd had finding him and getting him back home after desperately depositing an already frazzled cat at the cave door. She'd learned how vital communication is.

Contrary to their home's often busy noise, this quiet place was perfect for her to do her brain exercise. Lost in thought, she'd almost forgotten why she was there. Doing her brain exercise, she remembered.

She needed to figure out what would be the best action for all of them. They needed to communicate with each other regarding the known creatures.

She did, as you might expect, worry about her "be good to myself" treat. She just hoped the creatures didn't like honey. She was able to do her notice exercise after practicing her be-calm exercise.

It dawned on her that she hadn't breathed in a very long time. That was what happened to her when her fears began to grow with the feeling of fifty bees buzzing around inside her.

They buzzed louder, whirling faster, as the frantic wee bear remembered she'd left both defenseless Scruffles and Sweet Puppy out there with the creature. It was clearly time to talk to the maker of everything. Her courage needed to grow bigger than her fears.

When she heard the comforting humming of bees, she knew that the duo was safe. Everyone needed to sit down and do their brain exercise in a circle. It was time to tell all about the fog creatures.

She had to report that she'd been terrified because they'd been standing near her and hadn't noticed the cave wall shadow creature, and that she'd seen one at another time as the sun was going down.

That must be it. There were sunrise mist creatures and sunset wall creatures. Scruffles fessed up as they sat together in their serious mood that he had also been keeping quiet about seeing a mysterious large three-headed, ten-legged creature. Each antenna had a head and each head had two ears. At the very end of his story, he said the creature has a fairly fluffy tail.

Chapter 8

TO DESTROY OR NOT

Bea wonders why, when we see something different that we don't understand, we immediately fear it and promptly make plans to destroy it. She knew she did not understand this creature in the mist; it was clearly different than Sweet Puppy, Scruffles, and her. This unknown entity made her fears grow, and she felt like there were fifty bees buzzing inside her, but she wasn't sure what to do about it.

First of all, she had no right to destroy anything and had to admit that this creature had just as much right to be around here as they did. She didn't know the age of the creature or how long it had been there. It was possibly here first. She just wanted to do her investigation exercise to see if they needed to be afraid of it.

Recalling what her mom said about possibilities, who knew that this might even be a future friend? She remembered her mom's continuing bit of advice was to just be on guard.

It was settled. They would perform reconnaissance to do an investigation exercise. Since they had no idea how long this would take, being precise in her devising ways to learn more about the creature of the mist required intricate planning and packing up things they thought would be necessary, such as treats for everyone.

Scruffles wanted to drag a fish along with him. Sweet Puppy agreed to chew on that same fish. They had become very good at sharing. Bea made the gathering of sustenance the most complicated. She had to figure out how she could carry one of the clay pots of her golden "be good to myself" treat.

The smart bear made a note in her mind that she should ask Timothy to make smaller clay pots for situations like this. He had made some lovely pots, which he shaped from the mud along his pond, known as Timothy's Pond. They were edged with the imprinted patterns of his broad beaver tail. He set them to dry on a number of logs that he had industriously gnawed so that they'd fall from their standing position.

The wee bear could never carry a large, heavy clay pot like that. She already had to be honest with him and tell him one or two, or maybe three, had dropped and cracked. He'd reassured her that he, too, had cracked many pots. Bea did not need to feel guilty; she'd carried that heavy companion with her too often.

The proud wee bear nodded, admitting to herself that she had been faithful in doing her daily weight lifting exercise, carrying the honey pots up and down her step stool. She doubted if she was yet strong enough to easily transport one, especially if it were filled with honey. The concerned bear didn't quite know what she would do.

Chapter 9

A STICKY SITUATION

Scruffles wanted to slither silently through the tall grass. He hoped he would not run into any green or brown wriggling friends. They might startle him, and he would yowl and sabotage the whole exciting endeavor. But worse would be if Sweet Puppy barked.

This was covered very specifically during their orientation for the mission. Bea was very aware of what could go awry in this declared stealth activity. As far as the creature was concerned, she had no idea who or what they were dealing with. She knew very well, though, who would be accompanying her to accomplish this objective.

There were only a few exceptions to Sweet Puppy's rambunctiousness and poor focusing. One was when she smelled food; the other was if a chipmunk or squirrel were scampering around, then she would be devoted to tracking them. This would especially be true if they were anywhere within her vicinity.

Bea wondered what Sweet Puppy would do if she actually came face to face with a chipmunk or squirrel who wouldn't back down. That cute, pointy-eared dog would want to play with them. If she was met with resistance or any aggressive stance, she'd do an about-face and hightail it home. She might sluff off with her tail between her legs, feeling safe only as she ducked into their cave home.

Scruffles preferred to bask in the sun nestled in fresh-smelling green grass and posies. His favorite game was to dive, with his feet completely leaving the ground. An unsuspecting giant green grasshopper or a chirping cricket would be dangerously flicked at. Given this time, they would caper from blade to blade of grass, just a little more alert.

Bea felt certain she'd been thorough enough about possible situations that might arise. She was prepared for just about anything. We've been following Bea in her strolling exercises long enough to know there is always a surprise at the other end. Some outcomes are happy;others are not so.

It was the latter. Things went very wrong. What a disappointing disaster. Neither knew what the other was going through because they were silently screaming. Remember, this was a quiet search for the creature. Any sputtering, growling, or yowling had to be muffled. The entire effort came to an abrupt halt.
The only notice exercise Bea was able to do was see what a mess her entire body had become. She realized that she would need the others' assistance. As she looked around, her dread took over.

They were dealing with the same annoying, paralyzing situation. Scruffles was powerless to move with his two front legs fastened to each other. He was incapable of snapping his tail in agitation because it was anchored to his back. His whiskers each supported at least one burdock.

Instead of the 50 bees, it was just words buzzing in everyone's head. Burdocks. Burdocks here. Burdocks there. Burdocks were everywhere in their hair. Sweet Puppy's muzzle was a mess. Barely able to open her mouth, she was worried her teeth would never find their way to a delectable chicken leg again.

Bea was unable to raise her arms, paws, and claws to get the team's attention and to wave them in her direction. If they could laboriously inch toward her, she would motion for them to head back to their cave home. They could be seen, stuck to each other, downheartedly hobbling away from the sunrise and mist.

Chapter 10

STEP BY STEP

After swishing, swirling, tumbling, and plunging up and down in the river, they got most of the burdocks off. When burdocks get wet, the globes of clingers fall apart more easily. Unfortunately, each friend was pretty much on their own in the stream. By moving too close to one another, they risked becoming reattached. Each had to proclaim when they were completely clear of the burdensome burdocks.

Having dealt with that horrendous ordeal, they were able to focus on their next plan. To plan out the prevention of any further pitfalls, they'd have to travel in broad daylight to do an investigation exercise.

When they returned to that dreadful spot, they were relieved to see that there weren't many burdocks left. Most of the burdocks at this time, thankfully, were floating down the river.

Sweet Puppy, in pursuit of something living underground, discovered a large hole or deep pit at the edge of a grass-covered bank. Such a perilous abyss could have caused quite a commotion if any or all of them had fallen into that darkness. At least that calamity was curtailed. What could be left?

It didn't take long for the answer to that rhetorical question to reveal itself. They wanted to get as close and safely as possible to the path the creatures appeared to follow. Between them and their target was a wide swamp, through which they would have to muck their muddy way.

Doubts were doubling. Bea was beginning to do her brain exercise to gauge whether any of this was worth it anymore. It just seemed too difficult and complicated. Discouragement was setting in.

Summing up the courage to announce that she was calling the whole thing off was interrupted when Scruffles announced that he'd found a way around, over, or across. Without warning, he dove from the bank into the shallow edge of the swamp. Both Sweet Puppy and Bea were horrified; they would never employ that tactic. What could they do to save that rip-roaring raccoon cat?

They needn't have bothered to worry. That amazing raccoon cat was already in the deepest part. To their relief and surprise, he snaked in and out of the water all the way across. When he was safely on the other side, they all nervously laughed. Both Bea and Sweet Puppy's eyes couldn't have gotten any wider when they watched Scruffles' next trick.

He began slowly slinking toward their side of the swamp. Instead of leaping through the water, he pattered across the surface, dampening only the bottoms of his paws. He went in and out of their view. Most of the area he traveled through was blocked by weeds.

Before they could ask any questions, with their muzzles wide open, they listened to his explanation for such strange behavior. He told them he had done his investigation exercises while Sweet Puppy was sniffing out underground homes. He had noticed Bea was standing there doing her other-worldly thinking. She often traveled there in her head during her brain exercises when things were too challenging to figure out. We know that Bea was probably doing her talk to the maker. She had a need for courage and a solution. It appears the maker had heard her.

Scruffles told the story of how his head had bumped into something in the middle of the swamp, something hard. He judged it to be too long and too thin to be a fallen tree. With her eyes spying the area, Bea did her notice exercise and found no sign that Timothy had been there. There were no fallen trees brought down by a wood carving or clay pot-making beaver. So what could it be?

When Bea looked up, Scruffles was standing on the other side of the swamp again. He made no alarming splashing sound and was still barely wet. Strutting back to Bea and Sweet Puppy, the clever cat volunteered to show them where to place their feet, paws, and claws to cross.

He had just walked across an unidentified something that was concealed by the wringing wet ragged reeds. Bea did not want to get wet. She deferred the trying task to Sweet Puppy, who agreed to follow the wise leader step by step. Scruffles disappeared first. Sweet Puppy looked back at Bea with a desperate look in her eyes.

Fears were growing slowly. Had she made a drastic mistake? She had sent the two she was commissioned by the maker to care for into a dangerous unknown. Sweet Puppy disappeared next. Where had they gone? What had just swallowed them up? Bea could stand it no longer. She had to go look. To see. To understand.

Chapter 11

WALKING ON WATER

There would be no sunrise creature floating across the path this day. The intention was to get to the unexplored spot when the land was soaking up the sun. There were no burdocks to dodge, only a swamp to navigate. Bea had lost track of Scruffles and Sweet Puppy. They seemed to have shot across the water.

The wee bear decided to be brave enough to cross right behind Scruffles and Sweet Puppy. They had returned from the opposite side to help make her fears smaller. They reassured her that they would be with her every step she took into what she called the unknown. The two told her that the unknown would soon be known. This encouraged her to take those frightening steps toward the creature's path.

She knew, even though she felt like fifty bees were buzzing inside her and her fears were getting bigger and bigger, that she had to "take the plunge" for the sake of Scruffles and Sweet Puppy. She took her first fearful step forward, which was the only way to go. Preparing herself to feel her foot, paws, and claws deep in some mucky, muddy, sticky, swampy stuff, she was pleasantly surprised.

She opened her tightly shut wee bear eyes, and did her notice exercise. Peering into the deep, dark water, she realized she couldn't see anything that she could be walking on.

What was holding her up? Scruffles was right when he said it wasn't a broken tree underwater. She appeared to be walking on water in broad daylight. Still, she did not understand why her legs were not getting shorter. It didn't feel like stones; it was too smooth as she swished through the rough, rattling reeds, and she didn't feel it necessary to hop from one safe spot to another.

Here she was, in the middle of a swamp, doing her brain and talk to the maker of swamps exercises. This was at least the second most bizarre place that she had done these exercises. The first was when she was getting the tenderest twigs for Timothy the wood carving, clay pot making beaver, up a very, very, high tree. She had to claw her way down that rough, tall tree. That was something she'd never done before. Another learning adventure the maker would help with was finishing getting beyond the marsh.

She had made it without sinking up to her wee bear neck, somehow. As she touched sod, the wee, hungry, nervous bear disappointedly looked around, wishing that her "be good to myself" treat would magically appear. Her treat of golden honey, which her mom had introduced her to, would have to wait. But, oh, it would have certainly helped her think more clearly.

She usually did her exercises at least one or two times a day to get her clay pots of honey and be good to herself. Because doing her talk to the maker exercise was more important, she did that immediately.

Feeling better with that completed, she could now pay attention to Sweet Puppy and Scruffles. Facing their direction, she was happily greeted by the two, who joined a proud-of-herself bear. They were soon doing their water-splashing dance of joy.

Chapter 12

THE CLOUD LIFTS

Either the temperatures had changed quickly or the creature was late in its crossing. As the hazy mist rose and swirled, Bea was sure she had seen the head of a bear! Was the creature part-bear like Bea? Were those legs just like Sweet Puppy's?

Bea's mom had never warned her that there were such part-bear, part-puppy creatures roaming the land. She felt alone in this knowledge. They were unable to signal to each other what the other saw because they all knew they had to be completely silent.

As the cloud lifted before her very eyes, the fog dissolved into a bear carrying two small sweet puppies, with two larger sweet puppies following her. That is all it was? It was nothing to be afraid of? Just a mom with her puppies?

She didn't know what to do next, so she waited until the potential friends had completely disappeared beyond the embankment. Assuring them that their voices would not carry too far, she signaled for them to recross the water.

She couldn't help but wonder what was keeping her up from sinking as she skittered through the deep dark waters, hiding in the swamp mud. When they'd all gotten over safely, they decided to make their way back home to discuss what had just happened. Bea was not much of a conversationalist on their way back because she was preoccupied with her brain exercise.

Bea did a debating exercise in her head about this situation. This was another mom. They could help each other out. What if this mom did not want any help from Bea? What if she was happy just being by herself?

Bea remembered the rest of what her mom had said about this subject of possibilities. Sometimes you had to do the on-guard exercise and take the next step, even if the fears came back. And her bad memories of those mean little bears not wanting to be friends with her sure were racing back right now.

Chapter 13

WHAT-IFS

Bea had no excuse to delay a brief visit with this possible friend. Except when she thought of another bear like herself getting to know the real Bea. What if this mom did notice exercises too? Would she see her complications as well as the big and little mistakes she makes? Those fifty bees began buzzing inside her.

What if this new bear thought Bea was not a good mom? What if she thought Be Wee With Bea's exercises were silly? That would crush her like a flattened beehive that had fallen from a tree and been trampled upon. What if this bear wanted all of Bea's "be good to myself" treats?

How could she feed everyone? She didn't know where she could find enough fish. They already had to travel farther just to find a good fishing spot. Her thoughts swirled like the familiar waters in the stream where she and Scruffles had first fished.

Her "what-ifs" were winning the debate. She knew she needed to do her "be calm" exercise. It was time to do her talk to the Maker exercise. She wanted everything in balance, not tippy like trees that are half-blown over. She wanted to stop the old familiar "what-ifs," which she had practiced too often throughout her life.

She switched to practicing her notice exercise. The wee bear who wanted to grow wondered why her fears were stronger this time. She didn't seem as worried as was when she became friends with Timothy the wood carving, clay pot making beaver. He lived in the water most of the time. Timothy slept and actually spent his time in a dry area called His Lodge, but he had to swim a distance underwater to get there. Bea was not interested in undertaking new underwater swimming exercise.

Timothy and she did not have the convenience of getting to know each as thoroughly as this new possible friend and she could. Maybe that was why she felt safer. They had become very good friends, even though they spent little time with each other. This way, Timothy probably doesn't get weary of having her around and thinks she's fun. He wouldn't have bad thoughts about her. This new situation did not resemble her friendship with Timothy, the beaver, at all.

And this was not Willow, the patient and loving tree, only moved when the wind blew. She was great to visit when Bea had to talk about ideas that worried her and made her fears grow. This was a real bear mom with puppies.

Bea smiled, thinking about two moms working together and helping each other solve problems. She was doing well until her fears began setting in again.

How could they even possibly meet without this newly met mom suspecting that Bea had been following her? If Bea did her humble exercise, she'd have to admit that this thought wasn't too far from the truth. That settled it. She would not pursue this any further.

Chapter 14

A TERRIBLE HUMMING AND BUZZING

Something woke Bea. Bleary-eyed, she attempted to do her investigation exercise. She tilted her head; it sounded like a cave full of bees. Was her cave home full of her friends who had the same sound to their name as Bea? It made her think of how she got her name. Her mom had always called her Bear.

The sun was peeking through the slow rustling trees just above her and her mom's heads as they sat quietly. It felt like a lazy bear day; even her fears seemed sleepy. But Bea wanted to learn something new. She asked her mom to write her name so she could see what it looked like. She wondered if it had the same marks as the flat pieces of trees she and her mom had seen on their strolling exercises. Bea was having some of her sweet treat while her mom wrote BEAR on a broken branch. A golden drop dripped right on the letter "R." With her left paw, she grasped the big purple crayon her mom had found on the path during their strolling exercise. The wee bear printed what she saw: B-E-A. That became her name from then on.

That buzzing that woke her would be okay if they were making golden honey for more of her special "be good to myself" treat. But why would they all be in her cave home? Usually, as we know, a humming is a good sign for Bea, but this was a different sort of humming. It actually seemed to be coming from outside their cave. Doing her brain exercise, she knew this was not the usual source of the happy sound of humming. She was sure of that fact when both Sweet Puppy and Scruffles quickly curled curiously close to her. They didn't know what could be causing that terrible sound either.

When leaves and sticks came propelling into the cave, Bea's fears began to grow. She could hear crashing, cracking, and thudding, which grew louder as she crept closer to the mouth of their cave. The angry wind was whipping through the trees and tossing them around.

The humming ceased as quickly as it had picked up. Bea was relieved about a few things. One was that no trees had fallen on the cave, as when she was young with her mom. The other was that the wind, which had come humming in an angry way, had not stayed long. For once, her fears did not take over.

Everyone was able to finally get back to sleep, only to be awakened again, this time by a terrible buzzing. Bea knew instantly, as she did yet another investigation exercise, that the source of this scary sound was not bees at all. It wasn't the angry wind either.

Doing her brain exercise told her that this terrible buzzing had something to do with the terrible humming. She remembered how it had shaken them awake earlier. The worst sinking feeling suddenly came over her. It was deeper than if she had actually sunk to the bottom of the dark-watered swamp. There was an endless muddiness swallowing her up. Her fears were growing. But this time, it was not about her.

Willow's safety stabbed her in the heart. She was afraid that this buzzing was happening around Willow and that she was in great danger. Willow was the most incredible, caring tree Bea had ever met.

Willow told her a story of how children gathered around her to cry and be angry about people who treat them in cruel ways. Bea feared that the one who had helped so many over time was now in need of help herself.

Chapter 15

HOPE VS HOPE

With Willow's well-being as her focus, there was no time to do her stepstooling exercise. More importantly, there was no time for her to do her weight-lifting exercise or to have her "be good to myself" treat.

As she did her sprinting exercise toward the path that led to Willow, she did her talk to the maker of Willow trees. Her dear friend had to be okay. Bea did not know what she would do if she didn't have her to talk to. What would the sad, angry children do if they had no place to go to be listened to or to rant, rave, and cry?

The terrible buzzing became deafening as she grew closer to Willow's safe spot. She had dreadful doubts that there would ever be such a safe spot again. Her wee bear fur face was drenched in tears when she stood to stare at Willow's spot. She felt weak, as if her honey-filled legs were getting very squishy.

She remembered how Willow had told her that child after child would come to her hurting, physically and emotionally. This loving tree did not want to think of the betrayed children striking her with sticks. She'd rather think that it was the angry sticks cutting into her bark.

Mixed memories came to her about all of the healing talks she'd ever had with Willow—how much Willow had helped her and how she was holding dear the stories of so many broken children. What would they do without her? The buzzing was so loud in her head that she couldn't do her brain exercise to know what to do with all of her emotions.

Should she just stand there for a silent moment and do her humble exercise and be thankful for Willow being in her life? She did not know what to do. Should she choose to do her sprinting exercise toward Willow and put her arms around her scarred bark? Or should she do the celebrate-life dance?

When she did the first two, Willow expressed curiosity as to why Bea had been crying and had such a dark mood. Bea realized Willow had no idea what was going on. She was just being her calm self. She informed Bea that the children had told her some men were sawing up trees that had fallen during the storm. Ah, the buzzing did have something to do with the humming. Bea felt a moment of sadness along with Willow for those other trees. Letting out such a forceful gasp of relief, she told her that it had been a very long time since she'd taken a breath.

With her emotions at such a peak, all Bea needed was to have Willow ask her how she was doing. The wee bear unloaded everything that had been in her heart. She told her of the mist creature mystery. She gave a bear chuckle to herself.

The often-too-serious tree laughed at what the mist creature turned out to be. Shaking her bewildered head, Bea still wondered why a mom bear just like her and puppies just like Sweet Puppy would be so scary.

She admitted that she'd been doing her pretend exercise while performing her notice exercise. This meant making the whole thought of the possibility of a friendship with this mom bear go away. Willow just listened as she told her about all of her fears.

Because Willow said nothing, it led Bea to the real truth. This was a very different situation from Bea's efforts to try and fix the unfixable. She remembered how she used to try so hard to fix something that was not hers to fix. By not saying anything nor trying to fix her confusion, Willow was allowing the very distressed bear time to talk this through.

Bea did not always understand the meaning of what she was supposed to learn from her struggles. What she had just gone through was a big hint this time. She had been terrified to lose Willow. Talking to the maker of humble bears helped Bea figure some of it out.

She was afraid of what would happen if she made a new friend. It might turn into a very healthy relationship. Moms exchanging mom stories and helping with hints about what each did that worked sounded so nice. Maybe that mom even did the talk to the maker exercise.

She hoped that was true. Needing to feed and keep all those large and tiny puppies safe surely made it necessary. Bea was beginning to like her already and felt more confident that she would like Bea. With her happy wee bear eyes looking upward, she bet they would want to get to know Scruffles and Sweet Puppy.

Admitting to Willow how she actually looked forward to getting to know the mom and her puppies, she thanked the remarkable tree for listening. Scruffles and Sweet Puppy joined the worry-free wee bear in her celebrate-life dance.

With all that had happened in a short period of time, the wee weary bear checked to see if she had any energy left. Strolling toward home, thinking of the positive possibilities, she did a light dance step of hope.

Chapter 16

THE CONVOY

As they headed toward home after the terrible scare about Willow's livelihood, the wee Bea planner was already beginning to think of how she and the mom bear could possibly meet. Would she bring Scruffles and Sweet Puppy with her as she did her strolling exercise? Or would it be better to meet the new potential friends alone? Maybe she'd just tell the other mom about Scruffles and Sweet Puppy. What a choice to make.

Then she remembered what Timothy the wood carving, clay pot making, caring beaver had said to her. She'd frantically gone to him to ask for help. She and Scruffles had their initial problem after she'd invited him to live with her. Timothy reminded her she should have discussed with Scruffles what he wanted when he first moved in. Bea always needed to make everything work out right. Sometimes, she made poor choices.

She thought she knew the best way to do things, but it wasn't the only way. This time, she did her brain exercise to do things right. She knew what the nicest thing for everyone would be during such an exciting visit. She needed to ask Scruffles and Sweet Puppy what they wanted to do. Did they want to come along or stay home and find out what happened later?

As you may have guessed, Scruffles chose to remain home, basking in the freshly risen sun. And, of course, Sweet Puppy could not let this opportunity to make new friends go. The plan was to hurry in the dark to get ahead of where the happily revealed convoy traveled. Then they would linger as if "full of business" until the mom bear came along with her puppies.

They timed things perfectly. Not much waiting transpired after the delighted duo got settled to where their new friends would come along. They heard the usual chatter, with a bit of bickering echoing. The moment Bea had worried about and planned for would soon be over. Remembering the manners her mom taught her, Bea introduced herself and Sweet Puppy. She then welcomed them to the area. The mom bear announced herself as Doolie. The list of her puppies went from tallest to tiniest: Benny, Zoe, Annie, and Maddie.

Sweet Puppy was immediately enamored by Annie, who did not even bother to look at her. To escape Sweet Puppy's admiring advances, she kept weaving under her long legs. Because Sweet Puppy was so focused on making friends with Annie, she did not notice that Maddie was wagging her little nub of a tail. She was rollicking with a hippity-skip on her three very short legs.

As it turned out, Sweet Puppy and Zoe, a much more appropriately sized puppy, began playing with each other. Bea wondered if that was the first time Sweet Puppy had done her simply-enjoying-her-life exercise. She seemed so free at that moment. It did Bea's heart good to see this, knowing what a terrible life she has had.

It became obvious that Annie's real friend was Benny, who was white, fuzzy-faced, and very anxious. His jumpy behavior made Sweet Puppy a little "stand-offish" with him. She was going to have to do her brain exercise regarding this quite large puppy. Staying calm but alert, she knew she'd be safe.

Annie, who had a firm facial pose that resembled Winston Churchill, indicated that she felt more secure in her mom's arms. The reason for this became obvious to Bea as they exchanged ideas.

You may remember that Bea feels a need for everything and everyone to have a specific name. She wanted to listen a little longer to Doolie to know what to call her. This is so the maker can find Bea's friends sooner. If Doolie ever needed help, Bea was going to make sure she could be found right away by the maker.

The longer Doolie talked, the more Bea began to think that she would refer to her as Doolie, the wise bear. She wanted the maker of wise bears to be able to find her new friend, Doolie. Bea didn't think that Doolie was going to need help right away; she sounded quite wise.

Bea realized all of her "what-ifs" and fears were unfounded. She did not have to worry about needing to find enough food for that family. Doolie told Bea of a renewable source of food, especially chicken.

What a nice change that would be for all of them! Then she thought of Scruffles, who wasn't there.

A promise was made to introduce Scruffles to the crew later. Doolie then told Bea and Sweet Puppy more about where this chicken place was. Inquiring about the chance there would be honey too, Doolie replied with a resounding yes. This note of hope for different foods had come just in time. The fish they caught were more scarce in the areas closest to their cave.

Their meeting was a fragile moment. Bea did not want to broach the topic of her Be Wee With Bea exercises. She also did not think this was the right time to mention her talks to the maker of everything or the maker of anything specific. She didn't know why, but she was quite certain that Doolie did her talk to the maker often.

The sun had not only risen but was high overhead when they parted, agreeing to meet again. It took a bit of an effort to tear Sweet Puppy away from her fun with Zoe. Bea had to promise her that they would be able to get together soon. The two resistant puppies said their goodbyes.

Maddie seemed especially excited to hear that she would be able to spend time around Sweet Puppy again. When Sweet Puppy went over to say her farewells to Annie, she was pleased that she at least got a polite snort out of her. That. to Sweet Puppy, was promising.

When they had traveled a distance, Bea looked back. Was that a little step dance she saw Doolie doing? And wasn't Zoe prancing too? She felt such gratitude. It was time to do her talk to the maker of new friendships. Bea's bad memories were slowly fading. Her heart experienced a little thrill as she and Sweet Puppy headed home, dancing to the gentle swaying of the trees.

The Crew

Annie, Zoe, and Benny

Sweet Puppy and Maddie

Chapter 17

DASHED DUMPSTER DIVING

Sweet Puppy was getting tired of fish. Believe it or not, even Scruffles was bored of eating things swimming around in their river. Cats can be finicky, and Scruffles was certainly no exception. Bea and Doolie, her newfound friend, compared notes on what moms would and would not do. She shared with Bea a wonderful secret.

Doolie had discovered a new source of food for everyone in her family. Such information gave Bea a feeling of growing excitement. She was noticing the need for a brand new exercise that she would call "dumpster diving."

After retrieving the other two, the enthusiastic wee bear announced their next mission would be known as "Operation Dumpster Diving."

                          Be Wee With Bea

Scruffles and Sweet Puppy may have secretly rolled their feline and canine eyes.

Scruffles would be the lookout. Cats love to sit quietly, staring here and there. Sweet Puppy would get too distracted and would stray off after finding a chipmunk's trail. Scruffles could not have even a little cat nap while on this assignment. Sweet Puppy was commissioned to be the liaison between the lookout and the enterprise.

Plans were finalized; they would set out just before dawn. Doolie, the wise bear, had shown Bea the best path to reach the rear of some grocery stores. There was a big problem, though. She had not led Bea through the woods in the dark.

As we all know, things look different in the terrible darkness. It is much harder to identify markings seen in the daylight. Cautiously stepping their way along the untrod territory, they heard running water. Such chaotic sounds in the past had signaled to Bea that there was dangerous chaos about to erupt.

The troubled trio had no time to yell and warn each other. The ground beneath them seemed to give way, and they found themselves tumbling and tumbling, round and round. They heard sounds of snapping, crunching, cracking, and finally splashing. The last thing they not only heard but felt was water.

Bea's fears were growing even greater than they already were. She knew she had to do her brain exercise. Who would have ever thought she'd be doing her brain exercise in the middle of a black, swirling river in the dark?

She remembered saying the same thing when she was at the top of a hardwood tree, getting as many twigs as she could as fast as she could. She had volunteered to gather the most tender bark for Timothy, the wood carving, clay pot making beaver. The only problem was that she was at the tippity-top of the tree.

She'd forgotten to breathe the whole time she was clawing her way up and down. That memory reminded her to breathe while swishing, swashing, and swimming. She also remembered the most important exercise she had done on that escapade, besides tree climbing: she had talked to the maker of wee bears. So she immediately did that, adding to the list the maker of raccoon cats and the maker of sweet puppies. Still unsure if they all had the same maker, she mentioned them individually.

She did not want to lose either of them. It was her responsibility to keep them safe. All she'd wanted to do was provide them with a variety of food. Look at them now. She once again questioned how good a mom she was for them. Those sad thoughts didn't last long.

She knew she was a caring mom. She encouraged them to communicate with each other as she regained her confidence. This way, they would know where the others were. They continued to be carried endlessly, further along, to an unknown destination.

As she was about to reassure them that everyone would be okay except for being very waterlogged, she heard the water sing a sweet, peaceful song. She didn't know why, but she had the certainty that everyone would be safe.

Though she told herself to breathe, she had not taken a breath since they hit the water. There was one deep breath taken as she began plunging downward, but none since. When she did her be-calm exercise, she was able to do a very important notice exercise. The river was no longer a river. They had been tumbling and turning in the stream that fed Timothy's Pond. They were floating peacefully toward the dam. She was most familiar with this pleasant pond. Feeling more sure of herself, that shaken wee bear directed the exhausted, sopping survivors of this harrowing ordeal to shore.

Bea sounded two slaps upon the water after everyone had shuddered as much of the water and terror off from their trembling bodies. Neither a puzzled Scruffles nor Sweet Puppy knew of this ritual.

They were equally fascinated when they heard one resounding slap coming from over there, wherever that was. A beaver, whom they hoped was Timothy, surfaced and swam their way. They had heard about him and seen his work. They often used his clay pots and carved furniture. They all began talking at once to tell Timothy their trying tale.

This was no sudden intrusion on Timothy. Fortunately, to help them hide from their enemies, beavers tend to do much of their business at night. The rest of the time they spend in their den or lodge, a dome-shaped dwelling. Bea admires Timothy for being able to build such an architectural work of art. To keep Timothy safe at all times, Bea and he had agreed that she would sound two slaps and he would sound one beaver tail slap upon the surface of the soft, rippling water.

On their wet and weary way home, Bea's mind was whirring. It would be necessary to revisit in daylight where they had gone wrong. She thought it was vital while drying off. For now, they rest, restoring their energy and courage. This adventure was not even close to being concluded.

Chapter 18

THE RECONNAISSANCE

After a little time had passed, everyone had sufficiently dried and fluffed up. Bea, the very courageous wee bear, assured Scruffles and Sweet Puppy that she was undaunted about their mission of dumpster hunting for diving.

Shaking her paw, she announced that she would not be deterred and hoped they were still in favor of continuing the plan. She reminded them that there would be a smorgasbord of good food waiting for everyone. They would no longer sink their teeth into anything boring. She thought it would be best to bring both of them to do her investigation exercise and see where they went off the path the other morning.

She did her investigation exercise during their exploratory stroll, which Bea referred to as "reconnaissance." She realized that the anticipated markings and identifying clues could never be seen without daylight.

She'd have to think of some other way for them to know when to stop—
to make a certain left paw turn and keep veering in that direction. She
didn't even want to think back at that harrowing experience when
they'd turn right by mistake.

But how could she leave a sign for them to be able to see in the hours
before first light? This critical quest of dumpster hunting had to be
concluded before the crack of dawn. They did not want to be discovered
by wanderers.

She remembered while doing one of her strolling exercises, she came
along walls made from piling stones in different patterns. She wasn't
sure what it was at the time, but now it was all coming together for her.

The stones that struck her in a magical way were seemingly placed here
and there in the stone wall. But how beautiful they were—the color of
snow with a very shiny gloss to them. They were of different sizes and
shapes. Individual ones were planted at the bottom, the middle, and
some at the very top.

Strolling a little further along, she had seen stones piled to resemble the
new friends she had made at Timothy's Pond. To help her meet more
friends, Timothy introduced her to different-sized turtles.

Picturing back, she remembered that there were large flat stones with
four smaller rounded ones placed where legs or feet would be. There
was a long stone for the neck. She did a little leaping dance in her
mind, recalling the most magical of all. One of those beautiful white
stones was placed right where her turtle friend's head would be.

Strolling into another area, she puzzled over a line of small stones. Her wee bear eyes noticed how the stones in that row got larger. At the very end, there rested a sizable stone that she called a pointy nose.

That design made her think of her snakely friends. She liked putting "ly" at the end of the names of some of her friends. It meant she loved them: Dovely, Foxly, Snakely.

But the stones she was inspired by were small piles by trees. She wondered if they had been put there to tell someone when to stop or turn in a certain direction. That's what they could build, or rather, she would. Even though Scruffles and Sweet Puppy couldn't lift stones, they could rally her.

Boredom was quickly setting in. She knew she needed to keep their attention. Explaining why the stones were in a certain pattern, she felt confident these signs would work for them on their next attempt. Everyone was properly briefed to find the store with a dumpster located at the back of the two stores that were beside each other.

Remembering that Doolie had said it was the first store, a lump formed in her throat, and bees began buzzing inside her tummy. Arriving at a clearing, they saw in front of them three stores, all with dumpsters. She was very glad that Doolie had told her it was the first one. If Bea had done her brain exercise, she might have realized that "the first store" could mean a lot of things. But she didn't, nor did she do her notice exercise.

She looked at her two paws. One was the paw she had used to write her name the day her mom showed her how. The dumpster on that side was what she would label the first. Or did Doolie mean the store down there at the other end?

More bees were congregating in her no longer empty tummy. Soon, there would be fifty of them. She wondered if "first" meant the first one Doolie saw. She wasn't even certain which path Doolie used.

As we know, things never quite work out the way Bea plans them in her wee bear imagination. Is the last dumpster really the first one? Or is the first one the last? We will surely find out, along with Bea and the other two.

Chapter 19

A TERRIBLE SQUISHING

An expedition was scheduled for the next morning. Why was there urgency? We'll never know. When Bea gets something in her mind, then that is that. As we have noticed, her impulsivity has never turned out well.

Scruffles certainly could tell us about that. He remembers, like some of us, how, when his yowling woke her, she reacted without doing her brain exercise. He found himself being thrown onto the hard ground outside the cave.

They began their mission in the all-too-familiar darkness. Soon, all of the missed firings toward the desired target would become a much-needed misty blur in their past. Doolie, the wise bear, had told Bea of the treasure. She was sure it would hold something golden for a wee bear.

The reconnaissance had been successful. The stones she piled as markers prevented any further mistakes. If one couldn't find a marker, the other could. Fortunately, they all had amazing night vision.

Doolie had told her that the store workers left packages of chicken outside what they called a dumpster, so it was easy to capture. Scruffles and Sweet Puppy were drooling, and their stomachs were growling so loudly they were afraid someone might hear them. Bea was dismayed when she found nothing outside the deep dumpster.

Fortunately, there were little steps for her to fit her feet on as she climbed up to the edge of the tall metal box. This climb was actually nothing in comparison to the climbing she had done to get the tender-barked twigs for Timothy. As she did her brain exercise, it occurred to her once again that she had been doing her brain exercises under very unusual circumstances and in unexpected places of late.

Making it to the edge and looking down into the dark unknown, she could see nothing. The determined wee bear carefully let herself drop down to the bottom. Squish. While doing her investigation exercise, she saw that it was what we call a banana. She'd never seen anything like it. Attempting to step out of that, she stepped into a package of tomatoes. She was extremely uncomfortable with the mushy stuff oozing through her paws and claws. Enough was enough. She wanted out of this terrible situation. There were no steps like the ones outside when she looked for them.

She wasn't even certain that Sweet Puppy was still out there. Bea had been too busy doing the glop, slop, and bop. The only music that played very slowly and rhythmically in her head during that dance was "shsslushhh, shsslushhh, shsslushhh." She could only hope that Sweet Puppy had not become distracted by a chipmunk and raced off, following the trail while it was still hot. The frustrated wee bear wished for her words to pass through the thick darkness and fly up and out to Sweet Puppy.

Her only chance was to get Scruffles. She was feeling those fifty bees buzzing around inside her. She always felt them when her fears were great. To make matters worse, new light was too quickly creeping over the treetops.

Sweet Puppy had been there all along at her assigned post. She understood what Bea was saying and immediately headed off to fetch Scruffles. The frustrated wee bear was able to do her talk to the maker of wee bears. Shortly after the talk, she heard the buzzing of bees around honey, which was always comforting and reassuring.

But wait, the buzzing was not just in her spirit. They were in the dumpster with her. She followed the happy sound. By doing her investigation exercise, she traced the darting yellow specks to a jar of honey with a fairly good-sized chip out of it.

Tipping at just the right angle produced a golden rivulet of her "be good to myself" treat. For a minute, she was in her pretend world with no problems. But the length of the minute could only be measured by how full the jar was—not full enough, not long enough. She looked for more. She didn't care, at this point of desperation, what she had to drag her paws and claws through. That honey-loving bear was sure there must be just one more jar buried in there. She never had time to complete her search.

Sweet Puppy had been able to find Scruffles, who had already climbed to the top of the dumpster and was very bemused. He was looking down at Bea, who was covered with a smorgasbord of fruits and vegetables. This mishmash was not the buffet they had planned for and fantasized about.

Bea realized that Scruffles had gone somewhere else in his head for the moment. She gave him a little time, then instructed him to jump down to the bottom. She did have to admit to herself that she was a little cautious and worried that both of them would end up stuck at the bottom of this gloomy darkness.

Scruffles dove in, with only one goal in mind: to assist his stuck mom in reaching the top. Fortunately, when he stood, he was very tall. Lengthening her body the way she had to while reaching for a clay pot of her "be good to myself" treat, she could grasp the edge of the holes in the metal. She would pull herself up enough for Scruffles to be able to get under her. When he stood up, it slowly raised her to the next set of holes. Bea was able to reach with one paw and her claws, using the other paw to pull herself to the top rim of the dumpster. She then started worrying about leaving Scruffles at the bottom. But he was a raccoon cat and was already balancing on the edge beside her to make sure she could get out.

Her shaking legs were remembering climbing back down that extremely tall hardwood tree she had unwittingly climbed to help Timothy the beaver. She remembered how relieved she had been to be touching the ground.

Chapter 20

SWEET PUPPY TO THE RESCUE

Bea, the exasperated wee bear, stepped down from the dumpster and stomped her claws and paws to remove as much muck from them as she could. She felt relieved as she lowered herself to the ground, but sad when she noticed the ground had no dirt or grass. It was covered with the same black hardness that still covered Bea's Golden Path.

She remembered what she had said to Scruffles at that horribly devastating moment when the two discovered her tracks buried. The same was going on here. The tracks of all those who had the opportunity and privilege of walking on this land lie buried beneath the same gloom.

The thought that someday all of the mud for clay pots and topsoil for planting trees for Timothy would be covered with blackness made her cringe inside. Her eyes grew round with worry. The softest of fallen pine needles for bedding and other unnamed dirt paths would not exist any longer. She wondered how many dirt paths had been covered over and if any of them had been previously named.

She wondered if any of the stone pilers had paths buried beneath her feet. The concerned bear hoped very hard that none of the important piles of stones had been disturbed, moved, or torn down to make room for this dark deadness. She was also sad when she thought of how many trees and maybe even someone's cave were under there.

She decided it was time to end her sad wondering. Ready to move on, she realized that Sweet Puppy was not standing anywhere near her assigned post. She could see an excited puppy off in the distance, running toward them, tail wagging, with something in her mouth.

It was not a chipmunk. Bea had to admit that she was relieved about that. She had no idea what Sweet Puppy could have gotten into. As she got closer, Sweet Puppy slowed her pace. Very hesitant and resistant, she dropped the chicken leg to tell what she'd been doing.

Sweet Puppy had conducted an investigation exercise, determined that they would not return home until they had achieved their goal. She didn't want everyone to be disappointed once again. They'd planned and practiced for a long time, even doing a dry run that turned out to be a very wet one.

She mentioned wondering if three was one and one was three. That ingenious puppy discovered that was exactly what had caused the confusion, which led to a mushy, messy mishap. Neither Scruffles nor

Bea had any idea what Sweet Puppy was talking about. But they did see yummy chicken.

Noticing their confused expressions, Sweet Puppy explained further. Wondering if Doolie meant the last was the first, she investigated the farthest one. All kinds of foods are laid out for anyone to take without the need for dangerous dumpster diving.

She'd found a sled that was kind of torn up but would do fine for carrying whatever they wanted to collect. She cheerfully announced that she'd always dreamed of being a sled dog. Scruffles happily found quite a few packages of tuna, and Bea had several chipped jars of her "be good to myself" treat.

The official sled dog, Sweet Puppy, led the joyous group home. As they danced their way back, Bea licked the non-chipped side of a honey jar and was puzzled by how one could be three and three be one.

Chapter 21

GOING TO WILLOW

Led by the veteran sled dog, Sweet Puppy, Bea, and Scruffles made frequent journeys to the dumpster. Risking the danger of making new friends benefited everyone. Bea reflected with the other two on how difficult things had been before meeting Doolie, the wise bear, and her puppies.

There was often a struggle to catch the decreasing number of fish in their river. Bea, the mom, was worried her little ones were bored. She wished she could do more interesting activities with them. Scruffles, as you might imagine, didn't really care as long as he had a sunny spot on the ground.

They'd met new friends. It was wonderful to observe how much happier they were. The difference for Scruffles was that, while everyone was playing, he had discovered a delightful circle where the trees opened up. His day-long snoozing was warmed by the sun.

Doolie had shared how relieved she was. Her puppies' infighting had been replaced by new interests: Bea's brood. They were always together and had learned some of the Be Wee With Bea exercises. A few were strolling, doing brain exercises or meditating, and talking to the maker.

Doing their notice exercise, Benny, Zoe, Annie, Maddie, Sweet Puppy, and Bea agreed that Doolie was acting as if she were up to something. They decided to follow her. Maddie, with her three strong legs, was about to do her routine longer-journey climbing exercise. She'd heft herself from Annie to Zoe, and to Benny.

As the lookout for the investigation exercise, Maddie would ride atop Bennie's head. Calling for stealthiness with absolute silence was easier with just three. There was often a fuss with three more; therefore, Bea volunteered to carry Maddie in one paw and Annie in the other. She made certain to keep her arms far enough apart to prevent them from quarreling.

Not one of them had any idea where they might end up, nor how long it would take to discover where Doolie, the mom, was going and why she had been so secretive. Everyone's fears were growing.

Bea reassured them they did not have to go if they felt unsafe. They could call the whole mission off, or just a few of them could go and report to those left behind. The consensus was that everyone wanted to go.

Bea knew where Doolie was going. She could not figure out how Doolie even knew about that hidden, sacred place. How could Doolie have discovered it? Had she been followed on one of her strolling exercises? How dare she track a wee bear with problems?

Old feelings crept in. She'd forgotten them for a while. Had she made a mistake by befriending Doolie? What would she do without her companion? She would have shown embarrassment had she not been a wee bear.

Holding both Maddie and Annie, she did her humble exercise. All too often, when she was disapproving of someone, she found herself practicing the same unacceptable behavior. Upset that Doolie may have followed her, she was now following Doolie.

The other thought that occurred to Bea was that Doolie had discovered this place during her own strolling exercise. Bea was reminded that it was not always about her. Here she was, ready to throw a wonderful friendship away.

As they arrived at the place Bea knew they would end up, she was filled with guilt for even being there. It was not right to be eavesdropping. She should be happy that Doolie has found her friend Willow, the compassionate tree.

She signaled everyone to turn back. There were stubborn, dismayed, and puzzled looks. Why had they traveled all this way without discussing or quarreling, as they were wont to do? Didn't Bea know how extremely difficult the task of behaving was?

Chapter 22

THE FINAL STROLL

Bea thought maybe he would come back one last time, as she placed a bowl of Scruffles' favorite fish in his spot. She was about to leave this painful moment when she remembered how long it had been since Scruffles had returned the morning she had thrown him out. An unnatural, bone-chilling yowl had rudely awakened her. This time, he would not return.

She set another bowl out the next night, and the next. No raccoon cat pushing a bowl of tuna was heard at all. Only silence. Bea's bittersweet memories echoed, sounding along the cave walls in the sad, sad silence.

What a lovely last strolling exercise they have had. Bea noticed that Scruffles had been growing weaker and thinner than when she first met him. With no appetite, he hadn't been able to enjoy his "be good to himself" treat.

Bea knew something was wrong. Her fears were growing, and she felt an urgency to do her talk to the maker of raccoon cats. Because he had not ventured away from his warm spot in days, they invited Scruffles to get some fresh air. He hesitantly announced that it was time for his journey to the Bridge of Rainbows.

All three decided to do a strolling exercise, appreciating the music that came from their surroundings. Even though Scruffles loved chasing the crickets and grasshoppers, he admitted that they were his favorite sources of music.

For one moment, Bea looked in the direction of Sweet Puppy, who was sniffing out the fresh trail of an unknowing chipmunk. Turning back around, she saw the space where Scruffles had been standing was empty. He was gone.

As the two shuffled home, bittersweet thoughts danced through Bea's memories. She would cherish them. Lagging a little behind, Sweet Puppy was uncharacteristically silent. He must have already been missing some of the same things.

Bea and Sweet Puppy woke to the sound of rain at the mouth of their cave home, where Scruffles used to sit. Music of deep sadness was created as it struck the ground. They both sensed it. Not too much later in the morning, the rain slowed to a drizzle and ceased, with dark clouds beginning to clear.

It was time she and Sweet Puppy left the darkest, dreariest den of their cave home. There was no purpose in staying and just being sad and angry. Even though three was now two, they agreed it was time to do a strolling exercise. As they deliberately moved one foot in front of the other, they left the spot open where the large raccoon cat used to walk.

The mist was clearing over the land, and the sun was burning through. Beautiful colors arched across the bright, broad blue sky in front of them. That had to be how Scruffles got to the bridge her mother had told her about, Bea thought. This was the answer Bea had been waiting for—the reassurance that Scruffles had found his way.

She fondly thought of how Scruffles had discovered a secret path that crossed the swamp to investigate the mysterious creature of the mist. Perhaps wonderful Scruffles found a similar hidden path that led to the bridge that is surrounded by rainbows.

She laughed, thinking of their twisted speculations about what the creature was, where it came from, where it disappeared to, and why it crossed the same path nearly every morning at the same time.

It was bittersweet that she had more good memories than bad. All of the Scruffles adventures were flooding out into the light. If we make new memories that are happy, they might help replace our bad memories. She didn't think it would show wisdom to cover them over; they would still be buried in the memory dumpsters.

Those bad memories were just whispers since Scruffles, Sweet Puppy, Benny, Zoe, Annie, and courageous, indomitable Maddie came into her life. Then there was dear, kind Doolie, who was caring and understanding.

Bea did not want to make her sad. Doolie had already suffered a significant loss when she watched her beloved friend Allie cross the same bridge. Bea worried that telling Doolie would bring back sad memories. So she decided she wouldn't say anything just yet. She felt so lost. Maybe Willow or Timothy could help her find her way.

Chapter 23

MIDNIGHT HEART

The devastated wee bear knew she was going to need to see both of them as time passed. Firstly, she needed to be with Sweet Puppy and alone with herself.

It seemed to Bea that Sweet Puppy spent a lot of time looking for Scruffles. Bea started her talk to the maker of raccoon cats exercise. Maybe if she wished hard enough, Scruffles could slide right back down the rainbow and everything would be okay.

She realized while doing her notice exercise that she frequently wished for everything to be okay often in her day-to-day exercises. Maybe the maker would be able to tell Scruffles that it was all a mistake and that it was too early to cross the Bridge of Rainbows.

When that didn't happen, Bea became angry at the maker of everything because everything felt so wrong and out of balance. Until now, the spiral of good that her mom had told her about had been in balance. Would it ever be so again?

She knew that in order for Sweet Puppy and her to feel safe and hopeful again, she needed to persuade Sweet Puppy to accompany her to see Willow and Timothy.

During their strolling exercises, Bea did her notice exercise and observed that the champion chipmunk chaser appeared to have lost her spunk. The chipmunks were probably very relieved, but it made Bea even sadder.

She knew how much Sweet Puppy missed Scruffles. Bea heard her whining and whimpering in her sleep, which was something she hadn't done in a long time. There were no clay pots large enough or plentiful enough to hold all of Bea's sadness.

She hoped that Sweet Puppy would agree to go see Willow. Usually, Bea would go on her own, but she wasn't certain that she had the strength to make it there on her own. Sweet Puppy could help create a distraction from Bea's heavy sinking feeling. This whole experience required something rigorous, but she wasn't sure what it was. She felt so lost. Maybe Willow or Timothy could help her find her way.

After doing her stepstooling exercise and because Bea, the broken-hearted wee bear, was so upset, she did some major spilling. This made it necessary for her to do some toe-touching exercises.

Not wishing to waste any, this meant she could be further consoled by getting just a little more of her "be good to myself" treat. Bea knew she needed to do a rigorous strolling exercise and do her brain exercise.

Strolling more slowly than usual, she heard the sad music of the wind through the branches. This made her think of the dark music that was playing in her sad wee bear heart. This music was accompanied by words of pain.

Midnight Blues

My heart is full of midnight, I'm as blue as I can be

For my handsome raccoon cat had to leave me

His tuna bowl is in his corner, I haven't had the heart to throw it away

And there's the ball he found one day, to jump and run and play

He helped me when there was trouble at Bea's Golden Path

He even shook off his sleepiness without
taking time for his raccoon cat bath

When I found him, he had sticky matted hair

It was very sad to see him standing there

Oh, he became so handsome, that raccoon cat

He was so skinny, then not too fat.

Good thing he liked fish, and not my "be good to myself" treat

It would have been hard to find him something else to eat

He'd sit and do his brain exercises with me

Which made us both extremely happy

He liked dancing during our strolling exercise each day

Now, he's not here, he's gone, gone away

He saved me when I did my dumpster dive

Oh, I wish that he was here and still alive

When we did our "the creature of the mist" investigation

He worked very hard to find the creature's identification

He helped us get across the swamp, he had discovered a hidden bridge

I still look for him, hoping he's just up there dancing on the ridge

We were three, now we're two

Oh, dear maker of all things, what will we do?

My heart is full of midnight, I'm as blue as I can be

For my friend, Scruffles had to leave in order to be free

He said at "the Bridge of Rainbows", he will
be waiting for Sweet Puppy and me

Until then, we will live our lives as full as we can do for now

Practicing our Be Wee With Bea's rigorous exercises and learning how

To get beyond this terrible loss, we must do our part

To change the music from sadness to joy, we feel so deep in our heart

Chapter 24

GRIEVING WITH WILLOW

Sweet Puppy agreed to go along with Bea to see Willow, who stood there and listened without being distracted. This was very important to Bea. One of Willow's special features is that she is almost always in the moment.

Willow was remembering some of the children who have come to see her. Now she was storing Bea's pain to remember later. Bea's thoughts brought her back to when the maker of willow trees told Bea to tell Willow that she held the memory of pain, anger, sadness, and other feelings that are too difficult for most humans to hold.

It was a wonderful exercise that she did, remembering. Bea wouldn't need Willow to say much; she didn't want her to give any solutions or answers. Bea needed to figure things out for herself. Bea had begun to practice one of Willow's exercises. It was a challenge for Bea to let others figure out things for themselves. This required her to practice her "be humble" exercise.

She used to be a bit of a bully, like water that pushes its way around and shoves everything in its path. This was especially true when she first took Scruffles into her cave home. She never even asked him how he would like things to be for him.

Willow did tell Bea and Sweet Puppy to allow themselves to be sad for as long or as often as they needed to. If the sadness started and it felt like a big piece of something was missing, that was okay. It didn't need to be fixed within any particular time limit. She also said that the missing of one friend opens up the missing of others, such as her mom, and then maybe the bad memories will come back for a while. They won't stay, but it will feel like forever. This was precisely why Bea hesitated to tell Doolie about any of this. Bea admitted that she'd wondered why she'd been missing her mom even more since this had happened. Now she understood, at least a little bit.

The compassionate tree also told Bea and Sweet Puppy that they would have a mixture of feelings that would move from sadness to anger, to pretending or denial, to calmness, and back to anger and pretending. Courage and calm would begin to last longer. When will any of this happen? She could not say, it was just the way of it. Bea could see that Sweet Puppy was taking it all in. She hadn't said anything, although it was evident she was doing her focus exercise.

That was enough for that day. Bea could not do any more. The two could be seen strolling with a little more bounce than when they began.

Chapter 25

TIMOTHY LISTENS

Bea heard Scruffles yowling like he did when she first welcomed him into her cave home. She wouldn't throw him out this time the way we remember she did before, she promised herself. No matter how unnatural it sounded or how much it grated on her nerves, she would treat him differently this time. She'd let him get away with more, eat anything he wanted, and certainly let him go in and out when he asked. She felt better about it all now.

After she was finished with her pretending exercise, she began her investigation exercise. The mewling was Sweet Puppy whining and restlessly flailing her legs. It wasn't Scruffles at all. She knew Scruffles had gone to the Bridge of Rainbows. Seeing Sweet Puppy's angst drew her to wonder how she could comfort Sweet Puppy when she couldn't ever comfort herself. She had to do more healing exercises. She'd begun to do her stepstooling exercises, but even having her "be good to myself" treat didn't help.

She felt inconsolable. Nothing seemed to help her sadness go away. It was time to go see Timothy, the woodcarving, clay pot making, very patient and understanding beaver. As she neared Timothy's Pond, her sadness grew deeper. What if Timothy wasn't in his lodge? What if he were burrowed so deep that he couldn't hear her slap twice on the water to know it was her and not some predator? She stood there with her "if onlys" and "whys" and "no, it can't bes."

Timothy sounded one loud slap on the water with his beaver tail and swam to the edge of the pond, much to her relief. She was glad to see him because he would listen. It helped knowing he cared. She soon discovered he could understand her loss better than she had thought possible.

Beavers mate for life. Bea often wondered why he did not seem to have one. He never told her that he once had a mate. Timothy shared that, for some reason, his mate was dissatisfied with how he built the dam and lodge. He felt shattered as he watched her swim away, never to be seen again. She had broken the 'beavers mate forever' rule. He told Bea that a long time had to pass for him to get beyond that loss. It did get easier.

Bea was not reassured to hear about the length of time it might take. That meant more waiting, of a very painful sort. We know how little she likes waiting. Fortunately, going to Timothy's Pond was not a ritual she and Scruffles shared. There would be no reminder of Scruffles at Timothy's. It would have been harder to go visit him and she did enjoy spending time with him, except maybe the climbing-the-tree part.

She smiled to herself as she remembered how she had to do her humble exercise because she had been doing her pretend exercise. She had acted as if she knew all about climbing trees. We remember her giant fears as she slowly made her way from the tippy top to get the tenderest twigs to the ground.

Knowing he was able to have his favorite "be good to himself" treat made it worth it. She felt better knowing she could always come visit Timothy. This helped her realize she would find mutual understanding with Doolie. She would do her brain exercise on how to tell her about Scruffles.

Chapter 26

WITH DOOLIE

When Bea asked Sweet Puppy if she wanted to accompany her to Doolie's home cave, she was excited to go. With the wish that Annie would be more receptive to making friends, she planned to vigorously play with Zoe.

The other truth was that she didn't want to stay home alone. It was too empty there. They'd found another path so they didn't have to walk on water as Scruffles had taught them to do. Without Scruffles, who had gone to the Bridge of Rainbows, it wouldn't seem right.

When she met up with Doolie, she let go with unending tears. She told of Scruffles having gone down a different and final path toward the Bridge of Rainbows.

As Bea had anticipated, Doolie teared up and told her how sorry she was. Doolie still often missed Allie, her beloved puppy friend, who had also crossed the Bridge of Rainbows. Though the times had diminished, she admitted she missed her less often.

Not that she wasn't always in her heart, it was not a betrayal to Allie that she had moved beyond some of the sense of loss. She reminded Bea that she still had Sweet Puppy and that she needed to do her "be grateful" exercise. She cautioned Bea to take even more special care of Sweet Puppy.

Changing the topic, Bea decided to tell her about their adventure walking on water at the swamp when she had first seen them in the mist. Zoe and Sweet Puppy were the first to begin the trek across the dark water when they all went to do the investigation exercise.

Playing halfway across, the two friends went plunging into the rattly reeds and green scum. What a mess. But why are they no longer able to walk on the water? The next thing Bea saw was a definite wee bear head tilter.

Both Zoe and Sweet Puppy were back standing on the water, shaking themselves off. First, they were there, then they were not, and then they were. Sweet Puppy slipped while doing her shaking-off exercise, but still landed on top of the water.

This was a very puzzling swamp. The investigation exercise had to become more rigorous. Both Bea and Doolie dipped their feet, paws, and claws in the exact spot where Sweet Puppy and Zoe had begun stepping onto the water.

There was definitely something there to hold them up, but the water hid whatever it was. Bea thought of the puzzling exercises she'd done over her many passings of long sleep. In this case, there was no way to find out what held them up, therefore, it was a mystery they'd have to live with.

She had resisted and knew she needed to do her "detachment from things that have a hold on you" exercise. She always found that freeing. Why didn't she do it more often? Doolie said she suspected many others had the same tendency to avoid doing what is healthy.

What Doolie said next absolutely stunned and thrilled Bea. The wise bear said that she needed to visit Willow more often and began explaining who Willow was. Bea danced up and down and confessed she also visited Willow and how healing it always felt.

The other fun thing was Doolie called her Willow too. She was amazed at how right her mom had been when she said there are many potential friends for us to find.

Bea, the caring mom, smiled, remembering how sweet things had gone for the others. Maddie had a crush on Sweet Puppy who had no interest in her and Sweet Puppy had a crush on Annie who had no desire to give her any attention.

This time, Sweet Puppy was finding new friends. Just as Annie spent a little time with Sweet Puppy, so Sweet Puppy played with Maddie, whose little bob-tail rocked to and fro in delight.

For a day that had begun with such great darkness and loss in both their hearts, it had concluded with Sweet Puppy and Bea rediscovering their hope. They felt filled for the first time in a long time.

Chapter 27

MYSTERY SOLVED

Bea and Sweet Puppy often visited Doolie's expansive cave home. To be there, making new memories was easier than sitting in their old sad thoughts. Bea was telling Doolie of their first dumpster disaster and her two heroes, Scruffles and Sweet Puppy.

When told how Sweet Puppy had become a sled dog, Doolie laughed, adding Benny was theirs. Maddie enjoying an investigation exercise, finding a sled for them, had assigned Benny to be the sled dog.

As she was listening, Bea glanced at the wall in the room near the cave opening where Zoe and Sweet Puppy were tussling with each other. A could-be-frightening shadow creature moved upon the wall.

Practicing her brain exercise, instead of letting her fears conquer her, she learned something totally new. Watching the movements of Zoe and Sweet Puppy and the Shadow Creature, they were the same.

She decided she'd calmly mention this strange situation to Doolie who laughed. They had also experienced that fearful sight and ended up making a game out of it. With a demonstration, she explained how they played it.

Bea nervously laughed with relief that there was no shadow creature. As if a fog was clearing in her brain, she remembered what happened every time she'd looked away from the shadow creature on the wall in her cave home. She saw Scruffles and Sweet Puppy playing.

She remembered waving her arms and practicing her investigation exercise. She had become part of the Shadow Creature. Things were coming together for her. In her wild imagination, waving arms had served as the Shadow Creature's tentacles or antennae.

It all made complete sense. There was no such thing as a shadow creature. Scruffles would have enjoyed this discovery. He probably was laughing, dancing around the Bridge of Rainbows.

Bea thought it might be fun to make shadow creatures on the wall. She was anxious to tell Sweet Puppy about this potential game. Her mom had said that there are many potential opportunities for us to find. It just got to happen upon the right path.

Maybe this was one of the paths she and Sweet Puppy had been directed to take. They would learn that something scary could be changed into something fun. Going from fear to freedom, there could also be shadow dancing. She was beginning to like these ideas a lot.

Chapter 28

THE EVICTION

The sun would soon be resting, time to head home so they could rest. As the two strolled over the brow of the hill, Bea saw a strange flickering light. No, there were two. Now, three. The number continued to grow as she stood there doing her brain exercise. They were too large to be lightning bugs.

She loved lightning bugs, especially when they flew throughout the cave home, sparkling upon the walls of every room. Sadly, Sweet Puppy was afraid they were flashes of lightning from the booming crashing storm.

Bea followed with her eyes, the source of the shimmering light. The sun was shining directly onto puddles of something. But she couldn't imagine what it could be.

As she moved step by step closer, many golden slivers of moons began to take shape. Golden puddles. But not really puddles like mud puddles. These were a little up off the ground.

Doing her investigation exercise, she judged this all to be happening very near her cave home. Very, very near her home. Right in front of her cave. To the left of her doorway. The reason the puddles were a golden color is because it was puddles or rather pots of honey.

Some were just long golden-colored puddles with empty cracked pots tumbled in them. She planned to recover that spilled treasure later. The others were pots full of honey. She wondered who could have left her so many pots of her "be good to myself" treat.

She knew it was not Doolie, she'd just been with Doolie, Annie, Benny, Zoe, and Maddie at their cave home. With a combination of her notice exercise and a further investigation exercise, the clay pots looked very familiar.

They had the beaver tail imprint Timothy, the wood carving clay pot maker, had shaped and dried for her. Those were her own clay pots and the honey she had worked to collect. They belonged on her shelves which Timothy made for her. What were they doing out there on the ground?

When she and Sweet Puppy had left for their strolling exercise to Doolie's cave home, her "be good to myself" treat was safely in her eating room inside her cave.

There was her stepstool and right on top of it, very much out of its place, was Scruffles' precious bowl. She sprinted to see if it was all in one piece. She was so thankful that Scruffles didn't have to be there to see his happy home being ripped apart. Bea also felt ripped apart. What was going on?

Bea heard the wind play an ancient song through the grasses. Then she remembered the stories her mom had told her of how they had moved into their cave. She had watched it for quite a while and saw that no one seemed to be occupying it.

Bea, the devastated bear, had heard of the previous occupants and that they had been there over many long sleeps. She knew she needed to communicate with its original occupant, however, first, she wanted Sweet Puppy to come with her to check out a quaint cave she'd seen on one of her strolling trails.

The new find had not been disturbed in a very long time. They began clearing their things from the front of their now old cave home. Hoping it would someday feel welcoming, they slowly moved the few belongings to their new accommodations. The little scrapper, Sweet Puppy, wasn't sure if she thought this was the best way to handle such a crushing situation. Just to give in and move there?

Bea had done her brain exercise and had her talk to the maker and felt calm about the whole matter. This was the best way. There was no point in having a confrontation.

As they were standing there outside of what used to be their cave home, the new occupant came out and a tall bear introduced herself as Ona of this ancient cave.

She explained that over many long sleeps, her families had lived there until they had to take the path for their journey to the Bridge of Rainbows. She invited them to return to visit, however, Bea declined the invitation.

It would be too sad. That's where they had lived and grown and that was where Scruffles had curled up feeling safe. As they left, headed for their new cave, they promised each other that they would work together to make it a home even though three would now be two.

At least this place wouldn't have so many reminders of Scruffles. But she would always keep his bowl. If you did your notice exercise, you would see a bit of a slump in their step.

With fifty bees buzzing inside her, Bea practiced her brain exercise and her talk to the maker of cave homes. These exercises always made her feel calm. The comforting hum of busy bees told her she was doing the right thing and that this was the right cave for now. Even though she had no idea what the words 'for now' meant.

Chapter 29

DOOLIE'S STORY

Doolie offered Bea and Sweet Puppy to join her family in their cave home when she heard of their eviction. Bea thought that Doolie was very considerate and said she'd discuss the proposition with Sweet Puppy.

At this point, Doolie became very serious. Bea worked very rigorously to do her "wait in the silence" and "wait and be calm" exercise without trying to force a problem to come out the way she thought it should, not the way the maker knew would be best.

She needed to let Doolie talk first and not try to solve her problem. This was so hard for Bea to do, but she valued this friendship and did not want to demolish it like a clay pot falling from its highest shelf. She just listened, a new exercise for her.

Doolie said she'd gone to talk with Willow about all of her puppies. Each one had their own problems. Some even had bad memories which found their way into their dreams. She said she had heard whimpering on many nights and it wasn't from the same one or just one at a time. Willow had suggested that she encourage and accompany them to see her.

Doolie had told her puppies that Bea would listen in if they wanted her to, otherwise she would stand out of earshot. They loved her so much, they wanted her with them. She helped Doolie carry the little ones. Benny and Zoe tagged right along behind her.
Once they arrived at Willow's special spot, Bea surprised herself. She said nothing, but her mind was very noisy. There's a background story here that might help us understand what Willow refers to as she is listening and consoling each distressed puppy.

Doolie had cause for her own bad memories. Many long dark sleeps ago, Doolie was walking on a path that had a trick to it. Someone had spread brush all along it with some covering a deep hole.

Doolie had fallen into it and could not get out. The earth gave way with each claw scratch she made in her futile effort to reach the top. She knew it was urgent that she get out before the trap builder returned for his quarry. She began talking to the maker of bears to send help.

No sooner had she finished knowing that everything would be okay, when she heard a whinnying sound, up where the light shone through. To her amazement and great relief, a rope dropped down. No words needed to be exchanged.

She bit onto the rope and held on with paws and claws, and climbed painstakingly toward the surface. The predator would be disappointed and enraged.

In contrast, she was pleased and relieved. She thanked the beautiful multi-colored horse and promised she would repay her by helping another horse someday.

Chapter 30

ZOE AND BENNY'S STORY

This is where the puppies come into the story. And Willow did not miss pointing their strengths and abilities out to each puppy. They, on the other hand, were totally unaware of their strengths.

Zoe and Benny talked to Willow first. They shook as they spoke of their constant anxiety. Zoe wasn't sure what caused it, although she's had a difficult time when she was dragged out of her crate.

She had spent most of her life not eating much. When Doolie found her, Zoe was very thin and always experienced difficulty finding her appetite.

Benny also spoke of his anxiety. He had a food problem. He felt like he had to guard his food and wanted to gobble up any food he found. The others had to be careful around him and give him plenty of girth.

When they both told Willow about these causes of their distress and lack of confidence and composure, she reminded them of how they had been a great part of helping free Doolie from the cage she'd been locked in for helping free a captive horse as she had promised she would do one day.

The owner was enraged with Doolie and put her in the cage. Its lock was quite high up too. She told them they had been able to find their courage and calm to orchestrate the whole rescue plan. Zoe said they hadn't thought of it that way. There was such a load off their shoulders, they stepped more lightly.

Chapter 31

ANNIE AND MADDIE'S STORY

Annie and Maddie went next. They each had quite different problems, which created great discord in their lives. Annie told Willow she worried about her mom sometimes, and admitted she became very irritated and possessive of her.

She didn't really want to be that way. She didn't want to be as grumpy as she sometimes appeared or felt. Willow reminded her of how steady she'd been when Maddie had to crawl up onto her back to get to Zoe's back to get to Benny's head. Annie had such a nice feeling of contentment, maybe for the first time, Doolie thought.

Maddie became teary and pointed out to Willow that she had only three legs. She'd lost one when she got hurt in a place where people wanted to sell her puppies. She was sad about that too.

It was a dark hurt in her heart. But she expressed to Willow that she didn't feel that she could do much with only three legs, not as much as the others, anyway. Willow asked Maddie if she'd just heard what she had just recounted to Annie.

Maddie had heard everything but didn't see the connection. Willow reminded Maddie that she was the strongest of all of the puppies. Because she had only three legs, she had to work extra hard to do anything.

Her rigorous efforts had made her muscles more developed and stronger. Because she was the strongest, it was she whom Benny and Zoe commissioned to climb the highest. She had to somehow get herself up onto Annie's back, then up onto Zoe's back, and that was quite a climb. Zoe was tall.

Willow continued to describe to Maddie that she had performed the most difficult task of all when she had climbed up onto Benny's back, then up his neck to the tippy-top of his head to have to stretch and balance on her one little incredibly strong rear leg and stretch to her limit to lift the latch and to free their mom. Maddie had a strut to her hippity skip when she turned back toward the others. Doolie grinned as she told Bea that she felt that Maddie was going to be a force to be reckoned with after that adulation.

Doolie was so pleased with how Willow attended to each individually. She felt that they had finally seen themselves as she, their mom, had always seen them. They had discovered the first steps onto their paths in their search for hope.

Chapter 32

SHADOW GAMES

Sweet Puppy admitted Bea had been right to choose this cave for their home. It was closer to Zoe's home so they could play more often. Bea loved it too because it was closer to Doolie's home. They spent most of every day together when Bea was not tidying her home.

Bea decorated their little cave with the little trees she had begun growing when mud got tracked into her cave. Rather than be unsettled by the mud or disgruntled with the one doing the tracking, including herself, she just scooped it up, poured it into her empty clay pots, and planted some little saplings.

Their cave had a northerly opening. It made it a bit chilly when the wind blew, but it was lovely for the plants. She liked how the sun shone through just at the right time of the day. She placed some of her clay pots filled with golden honey a little lower on her shelves causing the sun to radiate off the honey. She had found ways to lighten up their little home. Sweet Puppy had found his favorite warm spot on the floor for long periods of napping.

She waited to see when the sun caused the shadows. She and Sweet Puppy would play the game Doolie told her about. While the sun was coming into their cave at the best angle, the wise bear and her puppies had great joy, without too much quarreling. Bea was excited to play with Sweet Puppy. She realized they hadn't played much at all since Scruffles had left for the Bridge of Rainbows.

First to go, Sweet Puppy's tail waggled just right to look like Snakely as Bea fondly named Snake. It didn't take an excited wee bear long to guess it. For her turn, Bea stood very tall and still, with her feet tight together. Her arms in different positions, she reached one up by her head and the other almost straight out. She could have been one of her favorite music makers that whispered to her on her strolls. She was a special friend. She was Willow.

Showing what fun they both had, when they finished playing, the happy duo shadow danced. Sweet Puppy thought they should invite Doolie, Benny, Zoe, Annie, and Maddie to play. They were prepared with good ideas to show them. What fun for all of them to dance and see wonderful designs that could be made.

Epilogue

Sweet Puppy enjoyed many warm hours of nap in her favorite spot on the floor. There were perfect places to store her chicken from dumpster expeditions, which they still went on without complications. Things were actually settling down for everyone.

Finding a suitable place to do her stepstooling exercise, Bea was beginning to feel the spiral of life was restored to balance. Things were settling down and making more sense.

Resting beside Sweet Puppy in the large circle of warmth, a lazy-feeling wee bear practiced her brain exercise, reflecting upon their many journeys. The right path had always revealed itself to her.

Doing her notice exercise, she was learning that much of her journey and the paths she was led to take were making her life better. She had found a friend she could trust and be trusted by, neither would knowingly harm the other. She had discovered new answers to old questions. These showed themselves to her whenever she practiced her Be Wee With Bea exercises.

Her gift of wisdom came from doing her talk with the maker and learning to be more wee and humble. She hopes everyone will practice these exercises, so they, too, will be able to discover the same kind of happiness.

Glossary

BRAIN EXERCISE

Serious thinking and/or meditation

STROLLING

Walking with great alertness

STEPSTOOLING

Going up and down a step stool to get clay pots of honey

FINE MOTOR WEIGHT LIFTING

Using the paw to lift gobs of honey from the pot to the mouth

TOE TOUCHING

Not wanting to waste a drop of honey, bending over to earnestly clean the gooey toes

FLOOR TOUCHING

Similar to toe touching except having to bend over further, to the floor

PUPPY or PUPPIES

The name for any dog of any age

BULLY

To taunt, call names, belittle by laughing, exclude from activities, emotionally pushy, often resulting in long-term trauma and emotional scarring

NOTICE EXERCISE

Really focus on what is in front of you, to really see things as they are, all done without distraction.